P9-DER-409

Hector and Prudence
ALL ABOARD!

by BRUCE KOSCIELNIAK

Alfred A. Knopf  New York

This is a Borzoi Book published by Alfred A. Knopf, Inc.

Copyright © 1990 by Bruce Koscielniak
All rights reserved under International and Pan-American Copyright Conventions. Published
in the United States by Alfred A. Knopf, Inc., New York, and simultaneously in Canada by Random House
of Canada Limited, Toronto. Distributed by Random House, Inc., New York.

Designed by Mina Greenstein   10 9 8 7 6 5 4 3 2 1
Manufactured in Singapore

Library of Congress Cataloging-in-Publication Data
Koscielniak, Bruce. Hector and Prudence—all aboard! / by Bruce Koscielniak.
p.   cm. Summary: Hector and Prudence and all their piglets set up the toy train under the Christmas tree
and go for an unusual ride.
ISBN 0-679-80486-2.—ISBN 0-679-90486-7 (lib. bdg.)
[1. Pigs—Fiction. 2. Christmas—Fiction.] I. Title. PZ7.K8523He 1990 [E]—dc20 89-20089

for Anne Schwartz,
who always has good ideas

A ll right," said Hector and Prudence to their anxious piglets on Christmas Eve, "there's one big present with all of your names on it. If everybody eats their peas and carrots, we can open it tonight."

When all the peas and carrots were gone, the whole family scrambled into the living room.

In a big box was a shiny toy train set. There was plenty of track, an electric power box, and even a cap for the engineer.

The piglets couldn't wait to set it up.

Ker-chug, ker-chug, ker-chug. The toy train puttered
around the track, making little puffs of smoke as it went.
"Oh wow! Neat!" said Berry.

"It's almost like we were going for a real train ride,"
added Terri.

"Almost," said Prudence, smiling.

"ALL ABOARD!" called Hector.
"Everyone, please sit down," said Prudence as the engine began to roll forward.

Suddenly, with Hector, Prudence, and the six piglets on board, the train was gliding through a snowy pasture full of cows,

zooming past frozen duck ponds,

stopping at a busy railway station,

puffing up one side of a mountain

and down the other,

cautiously crossing an old railway bridge,

always taking bumps in stride,

moving
swiftly
and
smoothly,

sometimes going in different directions,

avoiding trouble ahead,

never looking behind,

slipping quietly through the forest...

and finally rolling to a stop.
   "Are we lost?" asked Berry and Kerry.
   "No," said Hector, "we're home."

"Merry Christmas to all!" shouted Hector and
Prudence happily.

"And to all a good night!"